Window

Jeannie Baker

RED FOX

I am grateful to Haydn Washington, biologist
and environmental writer and consultant, for his help.

The artwork was prepared as collage constructions
which were reproduced in full colour from
photographs by David Cummings. The cover art was
photographed by Murray Van Der Veer.

A Red Fox Book

Published by Random House Children's Books
20 Vauxhall Bridge Road, London SW1V 2SA

A division of Random House UK Ltd.
London Melbourne Sydney Auckland
Johannesburg and agencies throughout the world

First published in Great Britain by
Julia MacRae 1991
Red Fox edition 1992

3 5 7 9 10 8 6 4 2

Printed in China

RANDOM HOUSE UK LTD Reg. No. 954009

ISBN 0 09 918211 4

To Rodney, Haydn, and David

AUTHOR'S NOTE

We are changing the face of our world at an
alarming and an increasing pace.

From the present rates of destruction, we
can estimate that by the year 2020 no wilderness
will remain on our planet, outside that protected
in national parks and reserves.

By the same year 2020, a quarter of our present
plant and animal species will be extinct if we continue
at the current growing pace of change.

Already, at least two species become extinct each hour.

Our planet is changing before our eyes. However,
by understanding and changing the way we personally
affect the environment, we can make a difference.

JEANNIE BAKER was born in England and now lives in Australia. Since 1972 she has worked on her collage constructions, many of which are designed to illustrate picture books but stand individually as works of art. They are part of many public art collections and have been exhibited in galleries in London, New York and throughout Australia.

Jeannie Baker is the author-artist of a number of distinguished picture books. Amongst them are *Home in the Sky*, an ALA Notable Book and Commended Australian Children's Picture Book of the Year, and *Where the Forest Meets the Sea,* which was an Honour Book for *The Boston Globe-Horn Book* Award and for The Australian Children's Picture Book of the Year, as well as the recipient of an IBBY Honour Award and the Friends of the Earth Earthworm Award. *Where the Forest Meets the Sea* has been made into an animated film, directed by Jeannie Baker.